NO FEELING IS

Gry Iverslien Katz was born in Oslo, Norway in 1952.
A photographer and writer who has lived for many years
between London and Andalusia. She has published
several books in England and Spain amongst them:
Impressions of Andalusia, Gibraltar and *Holland Park*. She is
also the author of a biography about the Norwegian
artist Joronn Sitje.

NO FEELING
IS FINAL

INSPIRED BY RILKE

A Love Story set between
Gibraltar and Spain
A Tale about a Young Woman,
a Poet, a Painter and
a Matador

GRY IVERSLIEN KATZ

ER
PUBLISHING

IN MEMORY OF

M. H.

*Believe in a love that is being
stored up for you like an
inheritance, and have faith that in
this love there is a strength and a
blessing so large that you can travel
as far as you wish without having
to step outside it.*

RAINER MARIA RILKE

I T ALL BEGAN WITH A GIFT from the Governor of Gibraltar's wife, a leather-bound book with gold lettering on the cover; Rose reflected as she thought back to the events which had led to her train journey to the mountain town of Ronda. Accompanied by her mother, she had entered a first-class carriage at San Roque, a village a few stops from the port of Algeciras in southern Spain from where the train line commenced.

Nineteen-year-old Rose Seymour was the only daughter of Major Laurence Seymour of the Gibraltar Defence Force and his wife, Anne, a piano teacher. The trip was to be her first outing for a long time. She had been ill, had in fact almost died, and her parents and doctor decided that she needed a change of scenery during convalescence. At first the plan had been to take her on a sea voyage to England, where they would stay at a relative's country house, a visit they could combine with a forth-coming family celebration. But Rose had begged them to allow her go to Ronda instead, a town in Andalusia that for centuries had attracted artists and romantic travellers. After much discussion, all agreed that mountain air would be more beneficial, and Ronda had the advantage of being closer to Gibraltar and the care of her doctor if needed.

It was late spring, and they had chosen an early-morning train before the heat of the day set in. The border crossing had gone smoothly – something that could not be taken for granted. Hostilities between British Gibraltar and Spain, ongoing for 250 years, had flared up once more after Queen Elizabeth's 1954 Commonwealth Tour the previous year, and Spain was again demanding sovereign rule of Gibraltar.

Mother and daughter had prepared themselves for a slow journey. Ronda was situated at an altitude of 733 metres above sea level and they would be travelling through rough, mountainous terrain with many tunnels and bridges, stopping at eleven stations before they reached their destination. The railway between Algeciras and Ronda followed the Rio Guadarranque in the lower plains, winding through cork woods, olive and orange groves and whitewashed villages before crossing ravines and passing towering mountain peaks. It had been constructed by the British in 1890 and was also known as the Henderson line, named after Sir Alexander Henderson, who had financed it.

There were some who claimed that it had been built purely for the benefit of wealthy travellers arriving by ship from England. More accurately, it was intended as a commercial line for transporting goods, a necessary and important gateway to inland Spain and Europe. It was also used by farmers and locals living along the line, and garrison officers and their families, to provide an escape from the claustrophobic atmosphere of the Rock. Two grand hotels had been erected at either end, the Reina Cristina in Algeciras and the Reina Victoria in Ronda.

Rose and her mother were the only occupants of their compartment, but the train was otherwise crowded, with a constant commotion of local farmers jumping on and off at the stations, laden with their produce and sometimes even with goats or sheep in tow. Half an hour into the journey, two *guardias civiles* entered to check for contraband. There were often smugglers on board, as might be expected on a railway close to the ports of Gibraltar and Algeciras. To Rose's great relief she and her mother were not searched, but through the door to the next carriage she could see two horrified nuns seated on slatted wooden benches being ordered to lift their tunics.

Mother and daughter sat opposite each other with two large suitcases close by, heavy with books. After her long illness Rose, a student of literature, needed to catch up with her studies. There was also a selection of the works of Rainer Maria Rilke, the late Austro-Hungarian poet and novelist whose writings Rose adored.

Her discovery of Rilke was due to serendipity, the fact that her name was Rose and because of Mrs Seymour's weekly visits to 'The Convent', as the Governor of Gibraltar's residence was known, to give piano lessons to her ladyship. One day, having told her pupil that it was her daughter's birthday, Mrs Seymour was given a present to take home, a bouquet of sweet-smelling crimson roses freshly cut from the garden and a privately printed volume of Rilke's *The Poems of the Rose*.

That evening Rose read the entire collection of twenty-seven poems that Rilke had written in his later years. She was instantly captivated.

> *Oh Rose, you perfect thing without compare,*
> *infinitely restrained*
> *and infinitely lavished, oh, head*
> *of a body with far too much wandering sweetness,*
>
> *nothing is equal to you, oh you supreme essence*
> *of this inconstant hour,*
> *your perfume wanders all about*
> *this space of love we have scarcely entered.*

The very next morning, Rose walked down Governor's Parade in Gibraltar's old town, past the grand building of the Theatre Royal and the statue of the young Queen Victoria, before arriving at the Garrison Library. It was housed in a handsome Georgian building set in a lush garden surrounded by orange and dragon trees. The library was a place she knew well and where she had always felt at home. The librarian found for her a slim volume of Rilke's poems amongst the myriad books. Upon opening it she discovered a double page showing the ghostly image of a woman which took her breath away. It was a faded watercolour by Auguste Rodin illustrating a poem titled 'You who never arrived'.

Rose sat by the train window watching the Andalusian landscape passing by. She was wearing her favourite blue skirt with matching blouse, and a tight belt revealing her slender waist. Her blonde hair was gathered at the back with tortoiseshell combs. A small cross of diamonds hung from her neck on a silver chain resting against her pale skin. She smiled to herself, remembering the gift of *The Poems of the Rose*, which had opened a new world to her and was now the reason for her journey to Ronda.

Rose observed her mother sitting opposite with a basket of oranges, purchased at the station, on the seat beside her. She complimented her on how lovely she looked in her chequered dress and her fashionable new straw hat. Mrs Seymour was reading the *Gibraltar Chronicle*. Even though it was late spring she was wearing gloves, to avoid soiling her hands with the newsprint. She looked up and smiled while proudly telling her daughter: 'After *The Times*, this is the second-oldest English-language newspaper in the world.' Rose already knew this, of course, but pretended to be surprised and impressed. Her mother added: 'At no point in its more than 150-year history has it ever ceased to publish!' Rose was used to the schoolmistress manner her mother had of trying to educate her, as when tutoring her through Chopin preludes on the baby grand piano in their front room in Gibraltar.

At no point had Rose been uncertain about her decision to go to Ronda. It was simply a journey she had to make. She felt great excitement about it, but also vulnerable and at a loss about many things in her life – not only about the disappointments and hardship she herself had suffered, but more about the effect her illness must have had on her parents, and their sadness upon discovering that she had been left infertile by the operation.

Overwhelmed by fatigue, melancholy and feelings of loneliness, she desperately hoped that a change of scenery and mountain air would restore her well-being. She knew her recovery would need time, and comforted herself with some words by Rilke:

> *You are also the physician who must watch over yourself.*
> *But in the course of every illness there are many days in*
> *which the physician can do nothing but wait.*

Rose knew only too well the meaning of patience, and she also knew that she was capable of great resilience. This journey was all that was now needed for her to return to life.

She thought of Rilke constantly. He had journeyed to Ronda in 1912, when he too had felt lost. Now, more than forty years later, she was travelling in his footsteps, on her way to the Reina Victoria Hotel, where the poet had also once resided. In which room had he stayed, she wondered? Had he felt depressed? Had he struggled to write? Had he been completely alone? Did he find solace there?

Although it was considered improper for a young woman to stay in a hotel by herself, Rose was adamant and eventually they had all yielded to her wishes. It had been decided that Rose's mother would settle her into the hotel, stay with her for a few days, and then return to Gibraltar, before sailing to England with Rose's father at the end of the following week. Their doctor in Gibraltar had made contact with a colleague in Ronda, Dr Sánchez, and the doctor's wife had kindly offered to come to the Reina Victoria once a week to have tea with Rose.

They stopped in the valley at the foot of the town, at a station called La Indiana. To Rose the name sounded like something out of the wild west and it increased her

sense of adventure as the train began its final ascent
to Ronda.

One of the most spectacular sites in Spain, Ronda was
situated on a plateau with panoramic views and divided
by a deep ravine. This made it a natural fortress and
it had therefore been inhabited since prehistoric times,
attracting a succession of civilisations – Phoenicians,
Romans, Moors and Christians.

At the station Rose and her mother were met by a driver
from the hotel. They were grateful to see him amidst the
commotion of people, animals and baggage, as well as a
crowd of hustling vendors with baskets of produce. Two
gypsy women charged towards them. They were selling
small bouquets of rosemary for good luck. One of them got
hold of Rose's hand and insisted on reading her palm. She
had to struggle to free herself before the driver managed
to shoo the fortune-tellers away. He brought the two
women the short distance to the Hotel Reina Victoria,
a large white building with dark-green shutters. Erected at
the beginning of the century and surrounded by tall pine
trees, it looked more alpine than Spanish. It was almost
perched on the edge of a precipice, only separated from
it by a small garden and El Paseo de los Ingleses, a narrow
walkway that ran from the hotel to the Alameda Park.
The magnificent views overlooked a large, fertile valley

of olive groves and surrounding mountains, peak after peak fading into the distance.

Excited, they entered the hotel through an attractive stone portal carved with garlands of Tudor roses and pomegranates, emblematic of the kingdoms of England and Spain. At the reception desk they were welcomed by the concierge, Señor Fernández, a jolly, red-faced man whose stomach was barely contained by his gold-buttoned waistcoat. As her mother was writing their names in the register, Rose whispered: 'Please ask him about Rilke's room.' Her mother did not respond, choosing to ignore her question.

The room they were given was small but attractive, with grey walls, pale-blue silk curtains, painted furniture, a small chandelier and an oriental-style carpet in the centre of the floor. In addition, there was a handsome fireplace and a writing desk by the window. A glass-panelled door led to a terrace that opened on to the stupendous scenery. Rose paused there for a moment and murmered to herself, 'I'm now looking at the very same view that Rilke once admired.' She felt happy.

First Rose unpacked Rilke's books, including the *Duino Elegies* and *The Notebooks of Malte Laurids Brigge*. Her favourite, *Letters to a Young Poet*, she placed on her bedside table, just as in her room in Gibraltar. It contained Rilke's correspondence with a young poet, Franz Kappus, in which he offered encouragement and advice concerning the mysteries of life. So many answers could be found in that slim volume that it had become her bible. The remainder of the books were left neatly stacked on the table.

For the next few days mother and daughter explored the town together, strolling through the Alameda Park, visiting the local markets and attending a service in a nearby church. While on their excursions they discovered the Fountain of Eight Spouts in the Padre Jesús district, where they cupped their hands and drank the cold, clear water. Thereafter they crossed the Puente Viejo, where the deep, dramatic cut of the gorge was in view, before ascending the steep cobble-stone road to the Salvatierra Palace.

They also paid a visit to Señora Sánchez, a kindly and unassuming woman. She took them to a local dance school to watch a group of young girls, including her own granddaughter, practising flamenco and learning to play castanets, accompanied by a young man in the corner of the room who played seductive tunes on a guitar. 'I find the sound of the Spanish guitar so enchanting. It evokes a desire to dance – to free oneself,' Rose whispered to her mother.

How exciting it was to be in Ronda, she thought, to embrace a culture steeped in history, so utterly different from the life she knew. Rose looked at her mother and felt gratitude for trusting her enough to allow her to stay.

'Try to write at least one letter a week,' Mrs Seymour suggested, as she prepared for her journey back to Gibraltar. 'If you feel unwell again, don't be heroic but please call on Doctor Sánchez. If you get very lonely his wife will come to see you twice a week instead of once.'

Rose found her concerns exaggerated, as usual, but listened dutifully and assured her that Señor Fernández would be there to assist her. Besides, the fact that she spoke Spanish would make it easier for her to engage with staff and fellow guests. 'Remember to do your exercises,' her mother continued, 'walk as much as you are able, but also rest and, last but not least, study. You will see that this stay will be life-changing for you.'

Rose asked her mother kindly to look out for new publications on Rilke while in England and to send what she found, if possible by air mail. Mrs Seymour promised to do so, then warmly embraced her daughter and added comfortingly, 'Remember, dear, Gibraltar is only a train ride away. No Atlantic Ocean to cross.' She lingered in the doorway for a while with a worried look on her face, reluctant to leave, but eventually blew her daughter a kiss and was gone.

Alone in her room, Rose sat down on the bed and surveyed the space that would be her home for the next two months. 'From today I will start a diary,' she said aloud to herself. 'I will buy a beautiful book to write in, a repository of memories that I will cherish later.'

Finding a handsome diary in Ronda did prove difficult, and she was obliged to make do with a humble notebook. She returned to her room in a state of excitement. There she saw her textbooks piled high on the writing desk; they gave her a pang of conscience, being the last thing on her mind. She pushed them aside, sat down and began to write.

'Ronda, 14 April 1955. I am sitting in Rilke's room and can hardly believe I am looking at the same view as he did when he arrived here in 1912.' Poetic licence, she thought – the fact that she had written 'Rilke's room'. However, since she planned to find out about that very room and hoped to move into it soon, she decided that it was an acceptable liberty to take.

Hours went by. She could hardly stop herself writing, amazed at how her pen ran along the pages almost of its own accord. Evening began to close in. Looking out over the valley in the sinking light, she added to her writings a section from Rilke's poem 'Pathways':

> *Understand, I'll slip quietly*
> *away from the noisy crowd*
> *when I see the pale*
> *stars rising, blooming, over the oaks.*

I'll pursue solitary pathways
through the pale twilit meadows
With only this one dream:
You come too.

No one, she thought, had ever written more profoundly about love than Rilke. Her discovery of the poem 'You who never arrived' had been a revelation. She knew it by heart and often repeated it to herself. It was filled with such melancholy, yet so haunting. *You who never arrived in my arms, Beloved, who were lost from the start.* She understood very well the meaning of these words. Why did she feel so connected to his way of thinking? She, being so young, so inexperienced, with only her longings and dreams. Yet the poem gave her a strange sense of déjà-vu, a vague feeling that she had lived before. It continued:

Streets that I chanced upon, —
you had just walked down them and vanished.

As a tribute to Rilke, the poem with Rodin's drawing had been framed and placed on the wall of her room in Gibraltar from the moment she had discovered it. She knew only too well how much he had changed her.

...All the immense
images in me — the far-off, deeply felt
landscape, cities, towers, and bridges, and
unsuspected turns in the path,

and those powerful lands that were once
pulsing with the life of the gods —
all rise within me to mean
you, who forever elude me.

The next morning Rose walked down the staircase from
the second floor, running her hand along the finely carved
railing, patinated by years of touch, amongst them that
of Rilke. Alone for the first time, she entered the elegant
dining room for breakfast but felt surprisingly at ease.
People were not sociable at so early an hour; this suited
her. She sipped her tea while planning her day, to take
a daily walk exploring the town, then come back to the
Victoria for lunch on the terrace before returning to her
room in the afternoon to study.

She looked through the window of the dining room,
over the vast landscape uninhabited except for a tiny
house perched high up on a steep point across the valley.
Later she asked Señor Fernández who lived there. He told
her his cousin had met the man once, an English painter,
but he did not know his name. He could be seen daily
crossing the valley on his donkey, which was usually loaded
with his easel and canvasses. He was making his way to the
Palacio de Mondragón. There, rumour had it, he was about
to start a painting school for English artists. Señor Fernández
suggested that on her daily walks she should try to find him
so she would have an English person with whom to speak.

Rose could not help it; her romantic fantasies immediately began to preoccupy her. What did the painter look like? Was he a young man? Was he an eccentric? A bohemian? A friendly person? How did he paint? However, without an introduction how could she, a young woman on her own, even dream of approaching him?

Taking a map and guidebook with her, the following morning she headed into town. She passed the bullring, which according to her guidebook was the oldest in Spain, built in 1784. The elaborate main entrance showed the coat of arms of the Real Maestranza or Royal Riding School, Spain's oldest and most noble order of horsemanship. A small crowd had gathered there. Announcements were being posted on each side of the gate, giving notice of the star attraction in the forthcoming Feria, a *rejoneo*, or bullfight on horseback, with the famous Don Alvaro Anozta. The billboard showed a drawing of the *rejoneador* on his white horse in full action at a corrida with a fierce black bull charging towards him. Rose knew the Spanish word for a bullfighter: 'matador', the one who kills. She loathed bullfighting and shuddered at the thought, the cruelty, so primitive, pagan – yes, simply barbaric.

She hurried on in the direction of Palacio Mondragón, through the Plaza Espāna, past the town hall, over the Puente Nuevo, a monumental eighteenth-century bridge with a 120-metre drop connecting the old and new parts of the town. She felt dizzy as she looked through the railing down to the deepest chasm of El Tajo, where the Guadalevín River ran and a few old buildings operating water mills were perched on the lowest part of the precipice. To the right side of the bridge she could see steep steps leading to a tiny room located inside the structure of the bridge. It had been used as a prison in the Civil War, from where, reputedly, many of the captives had been thrown to their death.

The streets of the old town were very quiet, almost empty. Following the winding road, she arrived in front of the Palacio Mondragón, which had once been the residence of the Moorish King Abomelic I. There she stood near the impressive main entrance, listening. Did she imagine the sound of a donkey approaching on the cobble stones? Could she hear the painter's steps? Could she feel his presence nearby? Might she see him behind the window-panes of the palace? Rose stood quite still, but all she could hear was her own breath and all she could see was her own shadow on the whitewashed wall.

Streets that I chanced upon — you had just walked down them and vanished.

Again she thought of Rilke and felt a surge of excitement. He himself had crossed this bridge many times and walked the streets and alleyways, stepping on the same cobble stones that she was stepping on now. 'Oh, how closely I can relate to him,' she thought, 'the way he uses words, his description of loneliness, his quest for love.'

Loneliness: she contemplated the meaning and thought about herself. No one would ever understand how she could spend so much time alone. But she did not mind, in fact she had always needed it, to be alone with her thoughts, her imagination, her books. Was it because she was an only child? Maybe she was different, or maybe it was because she had often been unwell?

In spite of her thoughts and her acceptance of solitude, she felt a little lost when she entered her room in Reina Victoria. For a moment she thought, 'Should I return to Gibraltar earlier? Maybe I won't get well in Ronda.' Her mountain retreat was a good place in many ways, but now she would have too much time to think and she was frightened that her melancholy might return. As always when beset with uncertainty, Rose turned to a volume of Rilke for comfort. There she read:

Perhaps everything that frightens us is, in its deepest essence, something helpless that wants our love.

The crucial thing was acceptance: to connect to the depth of your own being and love what you find there.

Lost in these philosophical thoughts, Rose had completely forgotten that doctor Doctor Sánchez's wife was coming to have tea with her. She rushed downstairs to greet her. Upon entering the drawing room with its large mirrors and silvery embossed wallpaper she reflected on how strange it was, in the most Spanish of towns, to be having neatly cut cucumber sandwiches and Earl Grey tea in an English hotel. This was her first rendezvous with Señora Sánchez, who had clearly dressed up for the occasion in a flower motif dress topped with a pale green bolero jacket. She was a kind but prim and a slightly irritating woman who treated her a bit like a child, and Rose was soon bored. She tried to talk to her about books but she kept changing the subject, so Rose decided that she probably did not read at all, and her mind began to drift. Surely there was no need for Señora Sánchez to come to see her twice a week, as her mother had suggested.

At breakfast next morning, Rose noticed that a distinguished-looking elderly gentleman was watching her from across the room. This made her feel uneasy, yet she was intrigued. She tried to guess who he could be and what he was doing in Ronda.

Although he was a stranger, she somehow felt connected to him as they were the only two in the dining room reading a book. At dinner the man was not there, but next morning at breakfast he was once again seated at his table reading. This time he looked straight at her and said, 'Good morning' in Spanish. As he left the room he passed her table and excused himself, saying his curiosity had got the better of him, and asked her what she was reading. 'It is a book of poems by Rilke,' she answered, curious to know his reaction, but his face was blank, as if the name meant nothing to him. She quickly added, 'He stayed in this hotel in 1912. He was a poet and a novelist.'

'Well my book is very different,' he said. 'It's about Francisco Goya's bullfighting *caprichos*, his etchings. He's an artist and it's a subject that interests me hugely. You see, there will soon be an important *corrida* here in Ronda – a *rejoneo*, and it will be fought by none other than Alvaro Anozta, who is the very best in Spain. He's a member of the Anozta family – the middle son.' It was now Rose's turn to look blank. 'Young lady, let me introduce myself,' he said extending his hand, 'Rafael De Lianza.'

'Rose Seymour,' she said with a polite smile.

'Oh, an English rose!' he exclaimed,

'No, I am Gibraltarian,' she hastily replied.

He raised his eyebrows and his expression changed as he gazed at her for a moment without speaking. Then he wished her a lovely day and was gone. She was relieved. She did not want to enter into conversations about bullfighting, an activity she found appalling. In any case, now that he knew she was from Gibraltar he would probably not be interested in any further conversation with her. Why did it have to be so awkward? Rose felt so much pity for the fortress Rock. It was so important strategically, and was therefore subjected to endless scrutiny and fierce disputes that constantly enraged people. She herself preferred to think of it in terms of Greek mythology: Gibraltar was one of the Pillars of Hercules, Jebel Musa mountain in Morocco being the other; together, they flanked and guarded the entrance to the Mediterranean. Plato had suggested that the area between them might be the very spot where the ancient city of Atlantis had been located.

The following morning there was a commotion in the hotel lobby. Señor Fernández seemed flustered, not at all his normal self. A group of guests and staff were keeping an eye on the entrance door. Suddenly Fernández exclaimed, 'It is him, it is him! It is Alvaro Anozta himself, the famous *rejoneador*. He is coming here for breakfast, he is meeting with Señor De Lianza!'

Rose sat down at her usual table in a chair facing the garden and the valley. She was curious about the *rejoneador*, and therefore tempted to sit on the side facing the door, to see Anozta's arrival. Shyness prevented her from doing so as it was not very ladylike to be so nosy.

His voice entered the room before him, loud, confident and deep, almost gravelly. Then he stepped across the threshold of the dining room like a thorough-bred horse entering an arena, Rose thought. No, he was more like a bull charging into the ring. Why did she compare him to an animal? He was not particularly tall, but his bearing was unusually upright and he was without question very handsome, and much younger than she had imagined.

Rose could not hear what the two men were talking about because their table was too far from hers. They had lowered their voice so much that she assumed they had to be discussing a private matter. At one point she looked up in their direction, only to discover they were both looking at her; indeed, they seemed to be talking about her. She blushed deeply, hurriedly gathered her books and left the room. His voice and his image remained with her all day. She was overcome by a feeling of breathlessness. In her room she lay down on her bed, worrying that this might have something to do with her recovery. It could not have been caused by his presence alone. She had never liked the 'macho' type, still less would she be attracted to a matador. That was another world.

Rilke was the kind of man she felt an affinity with, sensitive, creative, searching for meaning, questioning life, love, our existence, our solitude. Why was she so unnerved by a Spanish matador? She thought about the English painter and decided that the following day she would make her way again to the Palacio Mondragón in the hope of meeting him.

Early next morning, heading into town she passed a small barber's shop located within the exterior walls of the bullring and spotted Señor De Lianza inside. He was there maintaining his well-turned-out appearance, his brilliantined, swept-back hair and his finely trimmed moustache. The shop belonged to Señor Guerrero, who looked after bullfighters as well as locals. Posters announcing Don Alvaro Anozta's forthcoming *corrida* were everywhere – on the interior walls of the barber's shop as well as on the outside. The swaggering image of the *rejoneador* struck her as different now that she had seen him in real life. It instantly gave her a sensation of drama. She counted: only twenty-seven days to go before the *espetáculo*.

After passing the Convent of Santo Domingo and the hanging houses on the gorge, Rose soon stood in front of the door of the Mondragón Palace, observing life in the small square. She felt a little embarrassed, as this was the fifth time she had come to look for the painter. Church bells were ringing. A group of nuns hurried past, their gowns swishing and their headdresses making them look like a flock of birds as they walked to the convent in the nearby plaza. The palace seemed locked and bolted, without a trace of life within. A man repairing the shutters of a house opposite looked at her with curiosity. After a while she heard a donkey approaching. She held her breath. Could that be him? Would he speak to her because he recognized her as a foreigner? This would save her from having to approach him. A donkey's head appeared around the corner followed by its owner; an old farmer walking alongside trying to balance the heavy load, with two yapping mongrels following at his feet. Disappointed, she thought that maybe she was not destined to meet the painter, or that he had returned to England; there was no sign of him anywhere in Ronda. Maybe, even, he simply did not exist.

Exploring further the narrow streets and alleyways of the old town, Rose had begun to enjoy her walk. Then she saw a banner hanging from the veranda of a house with the words, 'Gibraltar belongs to Spain'. That dampened her spirits straight away. She hurried on and took shelter in the nearby Iglesia de Nuestra Señora de la Paz, a sixteenth-century church dedicated to the Patron Saint of Ronda. The doors were wide open. Once inside, in the cool darkness, she did not cross herself; she was a Protestant and that was not her custom. She went over to the devotional candles, rummaged in her shoulder bag for some coins, then lit one, and with closed eyes said a small, self-composed prayer.

Around the corner from the church, Rose had previously noticed a taberna where she had spotted a photo of Ernest Hemingway on the wall through their window. Señor Fernández had told her that the famous writer was a close friend of a bullfighting family called Ordóñez. Hemingway loved Spain and was completely obsessed with the *corrida*. Everyone seemed to talk about him and the Nobel Prize in Literature he had received the previous year. Rose had read his book about the Spanish Civil War as one of her literary projects at school.

Upon entering through the carved wooden door she noticed that the walls of the taberna were covered in pretty, hand-painted tiles with motifs from Cervantes' *Don Quixote*. The people in the bar stared at her and they all stopped talking. Rose imagined that it was not an acceptable place for a young woman to be alone. Nevertheless, she felt hungry and ordered some food: *patatas a la pobre*, little goat cutlets and some grilled peppers and tomatoes. She sat down at a table directly under the photograph of the famous writer and his friend the bullfighter, while observing people coming and going.

Suddenly she heard his voice, once again entering the room before him, and then Alvaro Anozta appeared in the doorway surrounded by a group of men and women. All in a jolly mood, they swept past her table and gathered at the end of the bar. Immediately plates of ham, cheese and olives were put in front of them by an over-eager waiter and glasses of sherry were generously filled to the brim.

The women were stunningly beautiful, exotic in colourful dresses with their manes of black hair and dark eyes. The men were loud and virile. They all seemed to flirt with one another shamelessly, and the women appeared to be particularly infatuated with Anozta. Rose felt pale and washed out next to them, almost grey in colour. Admiring the women, the poem 'The Spanish dancer' came to mind, and she tried to remember it:

> *her dance begins to flicker in the dark room.*
>
> *And all at once it is completely fire.*
>
> *One upward glance and she ignites her hair*
> *and, whirling faster and faster, fans her dress*
> *into passionate flames...*

Passionate flames, yes, that was how they seemed. They were so sensual, so spirited. She might be different, yet she knew only too well that deep inside her there burned the very same flame: unexplored, painfully restrained, at times both choking and exhausting.

Then, startled, she heard Anoztas' voice call out: 'Aha, the English Rose. *Salud*! Will we see you at the *corrida*?' Holding up his glass, he was looking straight at her. She responded with a nod, but by then he had already turned back to the others in his party.

It all happened so quickly that she wondered whether it had actually happened at all. The incident preoccupied her for the rest of the day. Of course, she felt flattered that he had remembered her from the Reina Victoria. He called her the 'English Rose'; she was glad to know Señor De Lianza had not revealed that she was from Gibraltar.

Later, her outpourings filled many pages of her diary. She was consumed by thoughts only for him. Would she chance upon him again? Would he come back to the Victoria to see Señor De Lianza? She knew that soon they would both be leaving town. Would it be necessary for her to go to the *corrida* in order to see Alvaro Anozta again? That was unthinkable.

To distract herself, she thought about the English painter and how she probably had much more in common with him, but also how silly it was to have such romantic feelings and fantasies about someone she had only seen twice, and to allow her thoughts to dwell upon an artist she had never met.

In the evening she looked across the valley to the painter's house from her window. Could she see a light? No, it was dark and deserted. Or was she mistaken? The window to the right seemed a little golden. Could it be a paraffin lamp burning on a low flame? Her mood inspired her to write down some of the most beautiful lines that she remembered from her favourite poem:

> *You, Beloved, who are all*
> *the gardens I have gazed at*
> *longingly. An open window*
> *in a country house — and you almost stepped out,*
> *pensive, to meet me.*

The next morning, she ran across Señor De Lianza in the hotel garden. He immediately began to talk about the *corrida*. She told him that she had seen Anozta in a taberna the previous day. Lianza replied that he knew, and advised her that in future it would be better if she had lunch at the Reina Victoria, unless she was accompanied by him. But he added nevertheless that the *rejoneador* had noticed her. He was fascinated by her porcelain beauty, and had asked Señor De Lianza whether she would like to join them at the *corrida*.

Choosing her words carefully, she said she thought it would perhaps be too dramatic for her. The killing of the bull would be upsetting, as she loved animals too much.

'Young lady, sit down next to me on this bench and I will educate you,' said Señor De Lianza. 'You see, it is man against beast. Think of a man riding out on his horse into a field and there he meets a bull; one of them has to win, one of them has to die. What you will see at the *corrida* is a rider and his horse in an exquisite dance with the bull. *The dance of life and death*. The bull is not just any old ox, it is altogether different: it is bred solely for fighting.

'Alvaro Anozta is a master of his art. His bravery and his horsemanship are the finest. I promise you: the death of the bull will be clean. Read Hemingway's book *Death in the Afternoon*. It captures the emotions of the bullfight as well as describing its rules and rituals. For bullfighting is not a sport, because the outcome is foreseen. It is a ritual.'

After he left, Rose could hardly believe that she had been involved in such a conversation. She had come to Ronda on a pilgrimage in search of her favourite poet. Her mind was preoccupied by themes of refined feeling and love. Now, suddenly, she was infatuated with a matador and she was about to buy Hemingway's *Death in the Afternoon* to learn more about his trade, the rules and regulations of bullfighting. He represented for her an alien world to which she did not belong.

Later, Rose found a letter that had been slipped under her door. It was from Señor De Lianza, inviting her to accompany him the following day to the Anozta family's *finca* on the outskirts of Ronda. 'It will be your first lesson in the art of bullfighting,' he wrote, as if it were a necessary part of her education. He had added a PS: 'There, if you are lucky, you might find a copy of *Death in the Afternoon*.'

She slept badly that night, constantly waking with thoughts of the bizarre situation she had been drawn into. It was something that every part of her rejected. Yet she had accepted the invitation. It was the only way she would be able to meet him again, the only way she would be able to confirm her dislike for what he represented and overcome her impossible infatuation.

Anozta's driver came for them the next morning. Heading out of town, they drove on a dirt track through kilometres of olive groves before arriving at the arched entrance to the *finca*. It was set amongst rolling hills. There were stable blocks located at the beginning of the drive, and behind them she noticed a small bullring, a *tentadero*. The main house had an impressive facade and large outbuildings on all sides which formed a kind of atrium.

As soon as they reached the front door Anozta appeared to greet them, accompanied by his stable master and two large mastiffs. On a shaded terrace to the right of the house servants were preparing a table with refreshments. It was the first time Rose was properly introduced to Anozta, who looked at her with an animated expression. A brief, polite dialogue between them followed, before the men eagerly engaged in their own conversation. Rose, ignored, stood by, silent and uncomfortable, wondering what she was doing there and what was expected of her. Their conversation even touched fleetingly on the subject of Gibraltar. She recoiled when she heard one of them say, 'Gibraltar will one day fall like a ripe pear,' but she remained silent. Her thoughts, on the other hand, lingered on that strange little melting pot, where people of all religions lived together peacefully. She wished she had the courage to tell them so.

After what felt like an eternity, Anozta announced that the stable master would show her around the property and take her down to see the horses being exercised. Rose understood immediately that the two men needed some time alone.

The stables were exquisitely well kept, with whitewashed walls displaying bridles, harnesses and saddles in pristine condition, arranged on brass pegs. A draught from the open doors enhanced the smell of the animals, which mingled with leather soap, polished metal and dry hay. The noble horses watched them curiously from their boxes, as the stable master introduced each one of them by name. Rose declared that she felt honoured to make their acquaintance, and said what a calming effect they had when she touched their velvety muzzles. Then she was taken to watch a young groom preparing a mount for its rider, employing a long lunge line to control the horse as it cantered in circles to warm up its joints and muscles. She was also told that this encouraged rhythm and helped relax the animal.

When they returned, Anozta asked whether she had enjoyed what she had just seen. She answered that she was overwhelmed by the grace and beauty of the horses, and that some of the techniques of dressage had been explained to her. 'I have a copy somewhere of *Death in the Afternoon*,' he told her, 'Let's go and try to find it.'

They left the main building and crossed a large patio at the rear of the house. The four corners of the space were adorned with potted plants, grouped together. In the centre there was a circular flowerbed that was badly in need of weeding and watering. She noticed, in the midst of the weeds, a single little rosebud growing on an otherwise sad-looking shrub. Anozta had spotted it as well, and he drew from his jacket pocket a folding penknife, cut off the rose and carefully sliced the thorns off the stem. Pressing the rosebud to his lips as he turned towards her, he then gently placed it in her hair. Rose felt faint and almost tearful by the beauty of his gesture. Neither of them spoke as they continued walking to the far building. He opened the door and stepped back to allow her to enter first. It was a large, vaulted room that was clearly used as an office and also housed a library. Rose was stunned to see the end wall of the room covered by the entire set of Goya's thirty-three *Tauromaquia* etchings depicting dramatic scenes of bullfighting.

Anozta, noticing that she was looking at them intensely, said, 'This is what Señor De Lianza has in mind to steal from me'; he laughed, letting her know that he was not serious. She made no comment, but immediately understood the significance of the book about Goya that De Lianza had been reading and the whispered meeting between the two men at the Reina Victoria. De Lianza was not merely a friend of Anozta; he was a potential buyer.

Still looking at the Goyas, she suddenly sensed him uncomfortably near. She held her breath, then felt a gentle kiss on the back of her neck. He was whispering, 'I would like you to come back here alone tomorrow.' Then, as if nothing had happened, he quickly turned away to search for *Death in the Afternoon* on one of the book shelves. Her hands were trembling when he gave it to her, and she clasped the volume tightly.

Back in her room at the Reina Victoria, Rose had to admit that the visit to the *finca* had not only failed to cure her, but she was now further entrapped. Hemingway's

Death in the Afternoon lay on the table in front of her, a book she would probably otherwise never have opened but now longed to read. She felt apprehensive, consumed by a sense of foreboding as she stepped over a threshold into the unknown.

As she entered the hotel reception the next morning, a beaming Señor Fernández rushed towards her. 'I am happy to say I have a surprise for you. Today we will move you to room 34, Rilke's room. I have found all of the notes about his stay here. He arrived on the 9th of December 1912 and left at the end of February 1913. Surprisingly, he did not even once enjoy a glass of wine with his supper, and the hotel charged him extra for wood to burn in his fireplace. He must have had a lonely Christmas! Hardly anyone stayed in the hotel that winter and there were days when Rilke was the only guest. Kindly prepare your suitcases so that we can make the change of rooms at lunchtime.'

Rose entered room 34 with a feeling of reverence and awe. She was finally standing in the very space where Rilke had probably written one of the *Duino Elegies* and many of his poems, including the wonderful 'Spanish Trilogy'.

First, she unpacked Rilke's books and carefully arranged them on the mantelpiece, together with a silver-framed photograph of the poet. *The Poems of the Rose*, the gift that had begun it all, she laid flat in the centre, and placed the treasured rosebud Anozta had given her on top of it. Then she randomly opened one of the books containing Rilke's writings from his time in Spain. Eerily, she had opened it to a page containing a letter he had written to a friend:

> *I have sought everywhere the city of my dreams,*
> *And I have finally found it in Ronda.*

I too, Rose thought, am dreaming of the place where I belong. But will someone like me find it here? Remembering the real reason for her stay, she was once again overcome by tiredness and melancholy. She had no hope of marriage. Since she was unable to have children, she was likely doomed to remain a spinster. Her life would probably be one of loneliness. She had endured so much sadness: her own bleak future and the sorrow this had inflicted on her parents, who worried that their only child would be alone, knowing they would never receive the gift of grandchildren. Rose continued searching through other volumes and read:

> *Be patient towards all that is unresolved in your heart.*

There was so much in her heart that remained unresolved, above all her desperate longing. She thought of Anozta and felt pain. Her infatuation for him was unbearable. If he knew her story, he would not waste time with her. She read further:

> *Make your ego porous.*
> *Will is of little importance,*
> *Complaining is nothing,*
> *Fame is nothing.*
> *Openness, patience, receptivity,*
> *solitude is everything.*

'Solitude.' Rose knew well the meaning of the word. She was the embodiment of solitude. She saw an image of herself alone in her room in Gibraltar with her books and records – her friends, as she called them. Strangely, she had always felt like an outsider from another world. She had found friendship with other children difficult and preferred the company of adults. Rilke had written beautifully about loneliness; this had been a source of comfort to her:

> *Embrace your solitude and love it,*
> *Endure the pain it causes,*
> *And try to sing out with it*

Her oddness had not been easy for her parents, who always seemed concerned about her. Soon they would return from England. Her mother had written in her weekly letter to Rose that she was planning a visit to Ronda as soon as they were back home. If Rose felt ready to leave earlier than planned, she should prepare to return to Gibraltar with her. Upon reading this, Rose became unsettled. Part of her did want to return, to escape, to run away from all that confronted her in Ronda. Away from feeling out of control, the feeling of danger. But what about him?

While pondering this question she closed her eyes. She often found she could see better that way. It added another dimension, a way to find answers from within.

Rose thought about her own parents' relationship; it was puzzling. Her father was strict and distant, a man of few words, always difficult to read and seldom at home. Her mother was playful, with a love of music, art and beauty. As long as she could remember they had kept separate bedrooms. Their only physical contact appeared to be an occasional kiss on the cheek. During her illness her father had said little and only gazed at her with sorrowful eyes, while her mother's concern was almost stifling.

No, she could not go back yet. She was just beginning to feel a strange sense of freedom, a freedom she had always longed for. Here in Ronda the air was so different, the landscape vast, inviting her to explore the surrounding mountains, hills and countryside. Going back to Gibraltar would now feel like returning to a cramped little prison.

For a long time Rose had wanted to cross over to the other side of the valley and climb the ridge to where the painter's house was. Late one morning she ventured down the steep steps to the right of the hotel which led to the bottom of the plateau. She followed a narrow path through olive groves, marvelling at the countryside and its abundance of wildflowers, dominated by marigolds and bright-red poppies. The stillness of the day was soothing, disturbed only by the occasional bark of a dog.

It took quite a hike, followed by a sheer climb, before she reached the top on the other side, but once there her efforts were rewarded by a most stunning view of Ronda perched upon the rock face of the *tajo*. She looked straight at the Hotel Reina Victoria and was able to locate the small veranda in front of her room. She then let her eyes glide along till she came to the bridge connecting the old and new town. Walking only a short distance further, she suddenly saw in the shade of some pine trees an easel with an unfinished painting. Bold brush strokes of hot orange and amber-yellow depicted the view she had just been admiring, but the artist was nowhere to be seen. Rose imagined that he had just popped back to his house for a bite to eat, so she lingered for a while, preparing herself for eventually meeting him. She had a strange fascination for this painter and she had even created an image of him in her mind. She looked at her watch; it was the lunch hour, then it slowly turned into siesta time. Rose waited but, alas, the elusive artist never appeared, and in the end she had to go back. She found the whole experience somehow unreal, but she laughed aloud at the thought of how much in the spirit of Rilke it had been.

streets that I chanced upon — you had
just walked down them and vanished.

On her return the concierge, Señor Fernández, was
waiting for her in a state of excitement, holding up a
parcel that he proudly announced had just arrived from
England with the postal train. Rose knew straight away
what it contained: her mother had succeeded in finding
a publication on Rilke. She ran up the stairs to her room
two at a time and quickly unwrapped a beautifully bound
volume of *Sonnets to Orpheus*, with a blue-silk ribbon page
marker which made the book look very exclusive.

Rose could hardly wait to show the new book to De
Lianza. He had become a friend and was now also a kind
of tutor to her. They had breakfast together each day and
then went on walks around town, usually discussing art.
About his own life he said very little, only that he was
not married or had children that he knew of. Rose had
taken to carrying a notebook, in which she jotted down
some of the things that De Lianza was teaching her. These
included stories about Goya, how the painter had been
a bullfighting aficionado in his youth, and when he was
older, in 1816, had made the masterly *La Tauromaquia*
etchings to portray the art of bullfighting. Rose in turn
introduced De Lianza to Rilke's writings, and he seemed
to be genuinely interested.

One day, when they were strolling through the San Francisco district of Ronda, De Lianza bought her some home-made marzipan from the Convent of las Franciscanas Descalzas (the bare-footed Franciscan nuns). It was a closed order, so the nun serving them could not be seen; the purchase had to take place through a small hatch in the wall, so all they saw was a slender hand, and heard only a gentle voice.

When they sat down on a bench in the plaza to enjoy the sweets, De Lianza suddenly revealed the reason for his prolonged stay in Ronda. As he spoke Rose thought he looked a little uncomfortable as if he was betraying somebody's confidence.

'I am a representative of an important art collector, and I am here to persuade the Anozta family to sell the thirty-three Goya etchings. It is rare to find a complete set and my client has ordered me not to return without them. To my disappointment, the Anozta family are willing to sell only a few of the etchings, but I feel that would be a great shame to break up the collection in this way. Negotiations are going back and forth, but we have not been able to reach an agreement.'

De Lianza continued speaking, now clearly more at ease as he generously informed Rose more about the Anozta family. There had been three generations of *rejoneadores* and they were known for owning the finest horses in the land.

The Goyas had been passed down through an aristocratic maternal branch of the family.

De Lianza made no mention of Anozta's love life, yet he seemed to encourage the flirtation between him and Rose. He often mentioned things Anozta had said about her: that he was intrigued by her, found her mysterious, loved her femininity, was mesmerised by her violet-blue eyes. De Lianza was beginning to act as a kind of a go-between, and he seemed to enjoy sharing their secret.

Rose felt a strange sense of excitement, but also urgency. She knew her time in Ronda was running out. Now that her health was so much improved, how could she justify the extravagance of staying week after week in a luxury hotel? She had been sent there to recover and to study, not to abandon herself to a romantic liaison. What did she have in common with Anozta, except that they were both young and flirtatious? Her rational side was not deluded about the probable outcome, but her heart continued to ache for him.

We need, in love, to practise only this: letting each other go. For holding on comes easily; that we do not need to learn.

Letting go. Yes, soon she would be returning to Gibraltar. She wondered what awaited her there. She also realised that it had been almost a year since Elizabeth II's visit. How well Rose remembered that day, her joy and tears at seeing the beautiful young queen walk ashore from the royal yacht. 'Long live our beloved Queen!' – the resounding cheers of the soldiers and civilians of Gibraltar were still ringing in her ears. They had no longer felt forgotten, but included. The queen's visit had been the most exciting and reassuring two days in Rose's life. Now she found herself in this strange and different place, ashamed of trying to hide the fact that she was Gibraltarian.

Anozta had been in Seville, but on the day after his return he sent his driver for her, with a note inviting her to be present during the morning session, the reason being that he wanted to prepare her for what she was about to see at the *feria*. He had already persuaded her to allow De Lianza to accompany her to the *corrida*.

As soon as she arrived at the *finca*, a seat was put out for her under a parasol, next to the dressage enclosure. Anozta was already riding his splendid horse Zeus, named after the king of the Greek gods. Straight-backed, proud-looking, deep in concentration, he controlled the animal with barely visible movements of his hands and feet, only the tendons in his forearms moving. His dark, wavy hair shone in the sunlight, his muscular body was tense. The grey horse was a stallion, but with its balletic grace and its long, flowing mane it seemed strangely feminine. Anozta appeared to be totally in control of the animal as it rhythmically stepped from one foot to the other and occasionally did a pirouette. Although Anozta never looked in Rose's direction, he must have sensed her presence.

She spent every day of the week that followed at the *finca*. The routine was always the same. She was collected at the hotel and taken straight to the riding enclosure to witness the morning practice. The stable master explained to her the techniques and rules, while she took notes and asked questions. Rose was particularly interested in the history of the noble, elegant horse and its working relationship with the rider. She was told that the Spanish thoroughbred was ideal for dressage, as it was known for being particularly intelligent, sensitive and quick to learn.

Lunch was always served very late, and brought out *al fresco* to be shared by all who were present, including the stable boys and grooms. The atmosphere was relaxed, as it was only young Anozta in charge of the *finca* during those days. Rose would watch him intently, his body language and behaviour, in an effort to know him better. He was always surrounded by people and constantly smoking his *tabaco negro*. He radiated self-confidence, almost arrogance, though he remained courteous to everyone.

There was a continual spark of flirtatiousness in Anozta's eyes when he looked at Rose; she was never alone with him, except when he walked his horse back to the stable and unsaddled and brushed him down himself. She would watch his beautiful hands, the way he handled the horse, so assured and so sensual. Rose felt overwhelmed by the feeling of how much she desired him.

Anozta's domination over the horse was total in the enclosure, but when he was not performing Rose discerned a deep and gentle love for the animals. He rode several horses, but with Zeus he had found his *binomio* – man and horse had become one. Sometimes, when Anozta approached the stable, he would call out to Zeus and the horse would answer him back. On one occasion she saw him lying in a field, resting in the warm sun next to his horse, and afterwards playing with him in the way one would play with a dog. Zeus followed Anozta around like a shadow, and at times gently brushed his head against his. The two seemed an extension of each other, their unity profound in their silent language.

Rose felt deeply moved witnessing the tenderness of such a close and mysterious bond between a human being and an animal. It made her fall even more in love with him.

> *Love consists of this:*
> *That two solitudes meet, protect and*
> *greet each other.*

How apt Rilke's words were, and how easily they could be applied to both animal and human relationships.

In the evening, when Rose was sitting at her writing desk, the direct view out of the window was that of the painter's house across the valley. She had stopped going to the Palacio Mondragón to look for him, although most evenings she would still notice whether or not there was a light in his windows. One day, when Señor Fernández at the reception desk told her that the painter had been spotted on the Moorish bridge, putting up his easel, she hardly reacted. The time had come to let go of him as he was no more than a mere fantasy. By now her thoughts were solely about her feelings for the physical reality of Anozta, who still had hardly made any direct approach towards her, except always wanting her near.

Then one day, when the horse was being unsaddled and Rose was gently stroking its neck, she accidentally touched Anozta's hand. He stopped what he was doing, took her hand in both of his and brought it to his lips, holding it there for what seemed to her like an eternity. Still it remained unclear to her what he wanted, beyond always having her with him, as if she were a muse. He had told De Lianza that he was fascinated by her porcelain beauty. But she was not made of porcelain. She desperately longed for him every day, but that, of course, was an impossible dream. Their worlds were too far apart, and for him she was probably no more than a curiosity.

Her world was that of life within Gibraltar. There her only experience of romance had been when she once held hands with a handsome soldier in her father's regiment. It had happened entirely by chance. The young man had been asked to guide her to the summit of the Rock. The path that led to the top went up the steep side and was known as the Mediterranean steps. The soldier had gallantly offered her his hand, pulling her up and later helping her down. She remembered the excitement they had both felt upon reaching the summit, like birds about to fly off to Morocco or Spain. They had shared sandwiches and drunk tea from his thermos flask. It was quite romantic, somehow, but he was on duty, and therefore it was left at that. It was strange to think that only a few years later she did fly away to Spain, where the hot, red soil nourished olive trees, where she was introduced to the world of horses, where she spent days in a *finca* amongst strangers after a chance meeting in a hotel, and where she had allowed her heart to run away with her. Now she found herself in a state of bewilderment and suspense, wondering what the outcome would be.

> *Who knows? Perhaps the same bird echoed through both of us yesterday, separate, in the evening.*

Late one afternoon at the *finca*, when everyone was packing up to leave, Rose told Anozta that her mother would soon be coming to Ronda and she would not be able to continue her daily visits. At first he looked startled, then he told her that his family were on their way to Ronda as well, so his days of having sole charge of the *finca* were also coming to an end. He took her by the hand and led her up to the house. For the first time they were truly alone. He began to ask her questions about herself. She was guarded in what she revealed to him, frightened that he might reject her if he knew the truth. Anozta looked at her intensely, the atmosphere was charged and her cheeks were flushed. It was getting late when, in a gentlemanly manner, he began to walk her towards the main entrance for her departure. Then suddenly, in a change of mind, he turned to her and said, 'Come, let me show you my bedroom.'

Afterwards, he laughed at her when she stood there in her crumpled dress and he went off in search of an iron. He told her, teasingly, 'I cannot send you back to the Victoria before you have straightened yourself out, as what has happened to you is all too obvious for everyone to see.'

Rose was totally overwhelmed by her experience, yet she wondered if Anozta would ever want to see her again. Was she just another conquest for him? He had not mentioned whether he wanted her to return to the *finca* the following day. Even so, she did not for a moment regret that she had given herself to him. She tried to write about her feelings, but could find no words to describe their intimacy. Instead, she found a sentence in the *Duino Elegies*, which she copied out in red ink in large, swirling letters in the middle of the page:

> *One earthly thing, truly experienced, even once,*
> *is enough for a lifetime*

To her surprise, at eleven o'clock sharp the following day the car arrived as usual. But this time it was Anozta himself who had come to pick her up. He looked happy and excited as he announced that, instead of going to the *finca* for the day, he wanted to take her on an outing to a derelict monastery, that of the Virgin of the Angels. As always, De Lianza would join them as chaperone. Rose felt that he sensed what had happened between her and Anozta, and seemed pleased.

They left Ronda, driving towards the sea through a wild and mountainous landscape. The steep, barren mountain passes gradually gave way to fertile valleys filled with orange groves. There were very few houses along the route, but eventually they reached a small village, and from there they turned onto a narrow dirt track that suddenly came to a complete stop. Through an ancient olive grove they could see the bell tower of the convent, with a huge stork's nest at the very top. The monastery was covered with ivy and moss, the grounds with bramble and rubble.

They entered the church, which had been looted and vandalised, left with gaps and empty arches on the walls where paintings of the saints had once hung. They noticed in the shadow behind the alter the serene-looking face of the Virgin, the only thing that had survived. It seemed the vandals had not dared to touch her, and they saw that a bouquet of fresh flowers had been placed before her.

Rose stood close to Anozta, her head leaning against his chest, listening to his heart beating in the stillness of the church. She was overwhelmed with emotions, remembering the way he had seduced her the previous evening, so gentle yet so passionate. She felt his closeness, his protectiveness, as they stood silently together for a few magical moments.

All of a sudden they heard a gentle voice singing in the courtyard of the cloister behind the church. There, at a well still in use, they found a heavily pregnant gypsy girl doing her washing. She was startled when she saw them, as if she had been caught out. Obviously, she was squatting in one of the deserted rooms of the convent. Rose chose this moment to reveal to Anozta that she would never be able to have a child. He listened and his only response was to hold her even closer. They left the shaded courtyard and walked, hand in hand, out into the sunshine without speaking. But Rose sensed that their thoughts were the same. Anozta's future was predestined. He would marry a Spanish girl who would give him many children, preferably sons who would follow in the family tradition and become *rejoneadores*.

De Lianza was waiting for them in the shade of the olive trees, where he had laid out a picnic. During lunch they told him about the gypsy girl who had made a home for herself in the convent and had placed flowers on the altar out of gratitude to the Virgin. On their way back to the mountains they stopped halfway, in a whitewashed village clinging to a mountain peak and dominated by an old Moorish watchtower. Anozta told Rose that there was something he wanted to show her and suggested that they climbed the tower. At the top Rose turned around and was met with a sight that took her breath away: there, across a sweeping, fertile valley, far in the distance, with the sea in the background glittering like an uncut precious stone, she saw Gibraltar, looking like a mirage or a giant sculpture. It brought tears to her eyes. Anozta and De Lianza stood in anticipation, waiting for her to speak. Rose said she had never seen anything quite as beautiful. On leaving the tower, they sat on the steps to the entrance and she tried to describe to them what it was like to be a colonial. She spoke about her father's position as a Major in the Defence Force, how he had been brought out from

England to Gibraltar at the beginning of the Spanish Civil War and how he had taken refugees into their home, giving them food and shelter.

And how later, during the Second World War, when Gibraltar reverted to a fortress and women and children had to be sent away, she and her mother had been evacuated to Casablanca. Rose told them of life within the Rock, how the family had settled there for good, she spoke about her schooling, her love of reading, her illness. The two men asked some questions but mostly they just listened. Only at one point did De Lianza interrupt, when he added in a comforting way that General Franco was presumed to have said: 'Gibraltar is not worth going to war with Britain for.'

That evening Rose wrote a full account of this extraordinary day: how Anozta had taken her to the watchtower to see Gibraltar, his way of letting her know that he had been aware of her secret all along, yet it had never stopped him wanting to be with her. She felt liberated, so changed somehow, after having found the ability to talk about herself and her life to two such attentive listeners. She ended with a passage from Rilke's novel *Malte*, which described so well the way she felt:

I am learning to see.
I don't know why it is,
But everything enters me
More deeply and doesn't
Cease where it once used to.
I have an interior I never knew of...

From that day on, their relationship had found a new level of intensity and they were hardly ever apart. De Lianza continued in the role of guardian, only leaving them alone during their most intimate moments. They were living every day to the full, clinging to time, time that was rapidly disappearing. Never once did they dare speak of the future they both knew they would not have together.

There were subtle signs of their imminent farewell. Rose's emotions felt confused one day when Anozta brought her to the *finca* to see a litter of mastiff puppies that had just been born. 'A souvenir,' he said as he placed one of them in her arms. She felt overwhelmed and sad at the same time, but told him, 'A large mountain dog in a small town house in Gibraltar would not be kind.' He did not try to convince her.

Their happiness was fragile, and soon the day arrived when Rose's mother was due the following afternoon and Anozta's family would shortly be settling into the *finca*.

After that, they would not see each other again until the day of the *corrida*.

The timing of her mother's visit could not have been worse. Rose had not yet come to terms with the enormity of what had happened to her. All she could think about was her lover and when she would see him again. She knew her mother would find her changed, but not in the way she had hoped. Besides, Rose, having totally ignored her studies, had failed to honour her part of the agreement. Her long stay in Ronda had not only been about regaining her strength after her illness; it had also been arranged to give her time to catch up with her missed work.

Instead, she had indulged her thoughts and time in a poet who was dead, a painter she never met, an elderly art historian and a young and very much alive matador. She felt ashamed of what her mother was about to discover. Maybe there were already rumours about her in the hotel? And what would Doctor Sánchez's wife, whom Rose had hardly seen, tell her?

But despite her anxieties, Mrs Seymour seemed quite unconcerned. She was merely happy to see Rose looking so well. She kept repeating that she had acquired an energy and spirit she had not seen before, which in her ignorance she put down to the clean mountain air. It was only the following day, after she had spoken to Señora

Sánchez, that Mrs Seymour began to look worried as she realised her daughter's stay had not been as innocent as she had hoped. She confronted Rose about the rumours of her involvement with a bullfighting crowd, and the fact that she had spent hardly any time at the hotel. Rose was prepared for such questions, and tried to calm her mother by telling her about De Lianza and his search for the Goyas, how he was a respectable elderly gentleman, an art historian from a well-known family in Madrid who had taken her under his wing to try to educate her about art, Spanish culture and traditions. Rose promised to introduce her mother to him that same afternoon.

The plan worked, to some extent. De Lianza managed to charm Mrs Seymour with his knowledge of music, and she was soon convinced of his role as a kind of elderly uncle keeping a watchful eye on her daughter. But this did not stop her from making a final effort to tempt her back to Gibraltar. She produced from her handbag an elegant invitation addressed to Rose. His Excellency the Governor of Gibraltar and her Ladyship were giving a ball at the convent in aid of the Red Cross. Mrs Seymour even promised, if Rose accepted, to lend her favourite off-the-shoulder crêpe de Chine evening dress. But to no avail. Rose was surprised to discover how little her mother knew her after all. She had never been excited by balls or dances, nor could they compare to what she was experiencing in Ronda.

With some cunning, Rose convinced her mother that, through De Lianza, she would now be able to write an interesting and unusual story about the history of bullfighting. She planned to offer the article to the *Gibraltar Chronicle* and it was therefore important that she stayed on and completed the project. Rose amazed herself by sounding so assertive, yet was regretful of her mother's defeated expression.

After Mrs Seymour had departed Rose was beset by feelings of relief mingled with guilt. She had to remind herself that she was now an adult, and for once she had acted like one. It dawned on her that she had lived a large part of her life in her mind, or through literature, reading romantic novels by authors such as Jane Austen and Daphne du Maurier. Now life had suddenly thrown her into real-life experiences that she had only ever read or dreamt about. Her parents would have to set her free, but, more importantly, first she had to liberate herself.

Rose thought of Rilke. He had prepared her for what had occurred. Now she would seek further counsel from his wise words.

> *I know of no other advice than this:*
> *Go within and scale the depths of your being*
> *from which your very life sprang forth.*

Rilke was with her again, always there to hold her, the spiritual father she had chosen for herself. She had underlined in pencil many passages in his books which had provided her with guidance, and covered many pages in the back of her diary with quotations from his writings. She would read them time and time again. Rose spent the next few days filling her journal with a love lament, not quite understanding why she had to be kept apart from Anozta. It was explained to her by De Lianza that the days leading up to the *corrida* were crucial and that Anozta should not be distracted from preparing himself for the big day.

Rose decided to use the time productively. Remembering the reason why her mother had let her stay, she sat down to begin her article about the history of bullfighting, which she titled 'Duelling with Bulls'. She explained that on the Iberian Peninsula in the eighteenth century, bullfighting had been a pastime of the Spanish aristocracy to show off their ability in horsemanship. It was a monopoly that could only be exercised with the permission of the king. Later the assistants of these knights began risking their lives by running with a cloth in front of the bull. This was even more dangerous than fighting bulls on horseback, and the brave men on foot soon became the stars of the *corrida* in their own right.

In the afternoon, while Rose was eagerly working on her article, there was a gentle knock on the door. De Lianza stood outside. He whispered that Anozta was in Ronda, having just finished lunch with the Marques de Valance at his palace in the old town, and he insisted on seeing Rose before he returned to the *finca*. Together they hurried through the streets and she was ushered into a side entrance of the palace, where Anozta was waiting for her in an anteroom on the lower ground floor. De Lianza immediately left them. Anozta passionately embraced Rose before leading her up the servants' staircase to a corridor on the first floor where the bedrooms were located.

The room was dark. Rose found herself drawn towards a window overlooking a sunlit terrace with a balustrade covered in jasmine; beyond she saw a valley that led her gaze to the pale blue of the mountains on the horizon. Anozta bolted the door behind them and gently pulled her back towards the darkness of the draped bed.

Afterwards, one of Rilke's sentences came to mind, which she adapted slightly:

They were lovers who had consumed each other like wine.

Anozta, lying by her side, seemed so peaceful; and so was she.

It was siesta time; Rose sat in the hotel garden sipping
lemonade, reflecting on the stillness of the afternoon.
She enjoyed feeling the warmth, inhaling the fragrance of
the geraniums, listening to the buzzing of bees and looking
at the expansive landscape before her. She felt in touch
with all of her senses, realising that Anozta had somehow
unlocked her, remembering their love-making, the
sensations, the vision, the sounds and scent from their
bedroom in the palace. Their romance, she thought, was
precious precisely because it soon would be lost. Instead
she imagined a room within herself, a place where she
could store these treasured memories, knowing she would
always be able to revisit them.

Her daydream was interrupted by De Lianza, who
had come to talk her through the events she would be
witnessing at the *corrida* the following day. Looking at her
curiously, he commented, 'You look different, you are not
a rosebud any more, you have blossomed.' She smiled and
said, 'Yes, I feel strangely transformed.' Then she quickly
changed the subject. She did not want to share the imaginary
space that she had been dreaming of. Instead, she gave
him her full attention, listening carefully and taking notes
as he spoke.

Bullfighting from the beginning symbolised the struggle
between the matador, who represented goodness in life, and

the bull, a symbol of evil and death. Today we no longer think of it in this way. Instead, the corrida has become an important cultural event. It is seen as an art form and part of our national identity. Tomorrow you will see what we call a corrida mixta, two matadors on foot and one on horseback. The three men will have two bulls each to fight, and they will be allowed fifteen minutes to tackle each of them, resulting in what we hope will be an outstanding performance and a clean kill.

Rose began to feel a growing sense of unease and told him, 'I might not be able to be there after all. Now it is not only the bull and the horse that concern me but Anozta and the dangers facing him.'

'He needs his muse to be there. You will bring him luck,' De Lianza replied.

'Then I must endure it,' Rose answered, before quoting the poet's words:

> *Let everything happen to you*
> *Beauty and terror*
> *Just keep going*
> *No feeling is final.*

On the day of the *corrida* the town was already buzzing in the early morning, with people arriving from far and wide. The hotel was swarming with guests readying themselves for the big event. The hotel staff were hard at work attending to everyone, in addition to preparing a celebration dinner which was to take place that evening in honour of the bullfighters and a select group of dignitaries. Rose felt relieved that her name was not on the guest list; De Lianza, on the other hand, was disappointed.

In the afternoon Rose dressed herself in a ruffled skirt and lace blouse, with a silk embroidered shawl thrown over her shoulders. She finished it off with a rose in her hair. That was De Lianza's idea; he told her Anozta would be pleased and honoured to see her dressed in the Spanish fashion.

Rose looked at herself in the mirror. Her lips were as red as the flower in her hair. Her breasts were almost visible through the fine material of the blouse. Her skirt was gathered tightly at the waist. The look in her eyes was intense and alluring, that of a seductress. She saw a woman she hardly recognised.

By midday the heat was already stifling. At five o'clock in the afternoon, the hour of the *corrida,* it would be at its peak. She was grateful they had been allocated seats on the shady side of the bullring.

Rose paused before leaving her room. She thought of Rilke and wondered what his thoughts and feelings about bullfighting would have been. Could he possibly

have seen some poetry in it? He would have passed the
bullring every day on his walk into town, but since his
stay in Ronda had been during winter he would never
have attended a *corrida* there. Suddenly she felt that she
was being unfaithful to his ideas of what was important
in life. Then she remembered some words he had once
written to Kappus:

> *Let life happen to you.*
> *Believe me: life is in the right, always.*

'Life is in the right, always.' What did he mean? Have our
choices already been made for us? Rilke had a profound
understanding of the human spirit, but was this his conclusion
— that everything was already somehow decided?

Her chaperone, the ever-debonair De Lianza, was waiting
for her in the hotel reception, with special invitations
from the Real Maestranza de Caballería de Ronda.
Both were dressed in their finery and they looked at each
other admiringly. Then De Lianza gallantly presented
Rose with a long, narrow parchment box; bewildered, she
looked at it, wondering what it could be. It was a daring
gift, as it turned out to be a painted fan with the images
of Goya's most famous pictures, *The Clothed Maja* on the
front and *The Naked Maja* on the reverse. The present
made her feel ill at ease; its significance did not escape

her, and was confirmed when De Lianza looked at Rose cheekily before offering her his arm as they began to battle their way through the crowds on the way to the Plaza de Toros.

The town was pulsing with fiesta spirit, the roadside was crowded with people, horses and carriages. The ladies were stunningly attired, in flamenco dresses in extraordinary colours and patterns, some with high *mantillas* adorned with lace and flowers. The horses were decorated in similarly extravagant fashion, and the men looked stylish in their starched white shirts and sombreros.

On entering the bullring Rose gasped at the beauty of the structure hidden within the outer walls, admiring the rows of ochre-coloured columns elegantly supporting the two-tier auditorium that could accommodate several thousand people. They were ushered to their places, facing the uniformed orchestra above one of the entrances. The musicians were already playing a *pasodoble*. The main gate was to the right. Anozta on his horse, together with the other participants on foot, would soon emerge from it to be presented to the president. Every seat was filled and the auditorium was a-flutter with cooling fans.

At five o'clock precisely there sounded a short ceremonial tune played on a clarinet. The spectators sat up in anticipation, facing the main gate. The first to ride in were two men dressed in black, in charge of rules and regulations. Then came Anozta riding Zeus, flanked by the two matadors on foot, followed by the *cuadrilla*, the team that assisted the matadors, carrying pink capes elegantly folded over their left shoulders.

'Look at him,' De Lianza exclaimed proudly. 'Look how splendid Don Alvaro Anozta Caballero *rejoneador* looks in his *traje corto* and his *sombrero de ala ancha*.' Rose was speechless and her heart was pounding. He looked spectacular indeed, and Zeus glimmered like polished silver in the afternoon light.

'I hope he gets a good bull, angry and strong,' declared De Lianza, 'so you can witness this excellent horseman's great skills and his bravery.'

'I can't understand why Anozta would subject himself to such danger,' Rose answered. 'I remember someone telling me once that to be truly brave you have to be truly frightened yet still willing to go ahead,' she added.

'For him the most nerve-shattering moment will be just before he rides in,' said De Lianza, 'when he is left alone for a few minutes in the small chapel directly inside the gates, praying.'

The arena was cleared and yet another ceremonial tune announced Anozta's return to the ring.

'He appears to be calm and controlled,' said De Lianza. 'What is not visible is his racing adrenaline and fear, but he thrives on the thrill of it.'

Anozta rode up to the president, removed his hat and bowed deeply, then galloped to the other side of the enclosure, where he crossed himself three times without taking his eyes off the entrance opposite. At that very moment the bull burst into the arena with great force. The members of the *cuadrilla* quickly emerged and began in turn to swing their capes to provoke the bull to charge. This was hardly necessary. He was already in fighting spirit, trying to attack the men one by one before charging towards the horse and rider.

As the teasing and the chasing began, the orchestra started up again, playing a melody that heightened the drama. Anozta seemed on top form, showing off his daring equestrian skills as he made the horse throw himself from side to side directly in front of the bull in an effort to confuse him as the terrified audience held its breath.

He came dangerously close to the bull many times, which enabled him to plunge several *banderíllas*, little harpoon-like spears, into its neck to weaken its muscles, in preparation for the final kill with a sword, called the *rejón*. At one point he even let go of the reins and steered the horse only with his knees, the spectators jubilant cheering him on and repeatedly calling out 'Óle'. So intense was the strain that it was necessary to change horses two or three times in the course of the allotted fifteen minutes. The first horse was jet-black. It soon became clear that this was an especially formidable bull, and Anozta quickly decided to change the horse to his dark brown. He was saving Zeus for last, when he would need all his strength and support to finish off the beast. At the moment of the kill he would have to be dangerously close and leaning precariously towards the bull. This required extreme precision so as to ensure that nothing went wrong.

As this dramatic spectacle proceeded Rose looked on with a pulsating heart and half-closed eyes, pressing her new fan so hard that the handle broke.

At no point in this daredevil situation did Anozta seem to lose control but, only halfway through, he decided to bring in Zeus, his most trusted mount, the horse to which he felt most attuned; the horse that meant so much to him; the horse with which he had been victorious on numerous occasions.

For the next few minutes they danced gracefully around the bull, side-stepping, pirouetting, even approaching him face to face. But soon it was clear that the *banderillas* were agitating the bull and it had become even more ferocious, tearing after the horse and rider, while Anozta continued to perform his perilous stunts dangerously near it.

Then, suddenly, Rose heard a great gasp from the crowd. Something had gone terribly wrong. 'Oh no, the bull got him! The horse is injured,' screamed De Lianza. Then she saw it. Blood was pouring from the horse's hind quarter, staining the yellow sand dark red, almost black. A commotion of *cuadrilleros* stormed out with their pink and yellow capes to distract the bull from the horse and rider. Anozta tried to steer the injured animal out of the ring. But the horse's legs were already failing, and he never made it further than the opening of the exit before collapsing, blocking the gates so they could not be closed.

De Lianza seemed to have forgotten about Rose as he sprang up and started making his way out of the arena. She soon caught up with him and followed, without knowing where he was heading. Once they were out of the bullring they ran to the back entrance and were let in through the first gate, but when they reached the entrance of the inner courtyard they were stopped. Through the railing they could see Zeus being pulled in. He was clearly dead. Anozta was nowhere to be seen and Rose panicked. De Lianza explained he was still inside. To maintain his honour, he was required to finish off the bull. That was the rule. Only a few minutes later he ran in and fell to the ground next to his beloved horse. It was heartbreaking to watch him cradling Zeus's head, sobbing.

Rose could hardly see through her own tears. She overheard some of the men in the enclosure talking. The horse's testicles were severed and this had caused a massive blood loss which gave him a heart attack. It had not been possible to save him.

De Lianza, ashen-faced, turned to Rose and said, 'I will have to bring you back to the hotel.' She did not know how to answer. All she could think was that she was meant to bring good luck to Anozta. As if reading her thoughts, De Lianza said: 'And I had imagined they were indestructible; this will be bad for Anozta, who will only blame himself for failing to protect his closest companion.'

With this the curtain has come down, Rose said to herself. She had known all along that what had begun eventually would come to an end. Nevertheless, she felt the end had come too soon. I might as well be the horse, she thought, as the separation from Anozta will make me feel like dying. Now everything seemed so final. She turned around to look at Anozta for the last time, but he was hidden by a wall of men who had gathered around him. De Lianza, visibly shaken, murmured, 'With this, everything has changed. The celebration dinner will still go ahead, but I doubt that Anozta will attend. His family are here and they will return with him back to the *finca,* to mourn the loss of their most precious horse.'

'And I will prepare for my journey back to Gibraltar, maybe as soon as tomorrow. I find it impossible for me to remain here for even one more day,' Rose replied. 'I won't be able to see him, and even if I did the farewell would be too painful. There is no time to inform my parents, so I will simply have to travel alone.'

Once she was back in her room, Rose crawled into bed feeling terribly lost and profoundly sad. Never again would she hear Anozta's voice or feel his touch. Their time together had been no more than an intense fleeting encounter. She reached for the book from her bedside table, *Letters to a Young Poet*, and held it. Between these covers, she thought, I will find something that will give me solace and hope. Who am I, but a composite of all my experiences? I am all the books that I have read, my deep connection to nature, the music and art that I have admired. I am my illness, my pains, my loneliness, my longings and the love I have given and received. She opened the book and there it was, Rilke's advice to Kappus when his love had abandoned him:

see instead that the space around you is beginning to grow vast

Her world had indeed expanded, and furthermore she had been changed and matured by her experiences. Continuing to search through the texts, she found another passage that had always intrigued her:

be patient towards all that is unsolved in your heart
and try to love the questions themselves, like locked rooms
and like books that are written in a foreign language.
Do not seek the answers now, that cannot be given to you
because you cannot live them. The importance is to live
everything. Live the questions now. Then perhaps you will

slowly, without noticing it, live the answer some distant
day in the future.

Rose meditated on his words: 'If I understand correctly what Rilke is saying, then everything is of value as preparation for what is to come. There is no quick way, but a steady and meaningful process, whereby everything has equal importance for the outcome that awaits one?'

The sunset that evening had turned the sky blood-red, more dramatic than she had ever seen it before. At one point the valley looked as if it were engulfed by flames, before the night sky suddenly changed to deep amethyst.

When the room was almost in darkness, Rose brought her suitcases down from the top of the wardrobe and began slowly to pack the books from the mantelpiece. Her journey had come to an end.

De Lianza accompanied her to the train station the next day. They both felt too sad to speak. He himself would soon be returning home, in low spirits and without having accomplished his mission of securing the Goyas for his client. Although neither said so, it was unlikely that they would ever see each other again. Their time together in the mountains had only been a short interlude in their lives, but it would be treasured nevertheless. Just before boarding the train Rose gave De Lianza a letter she had written to Anozta, which he promised to deliver the same day.

She was glad the journey would be slow. She needed time to absorb her experiences and gather her thoughts. She would not be able to talk to anyone as yet, she did not want to have to explain or be judged. What had happened to her, she felt, was simply too sacred for her to share.

The train was transporting her from one life to another, but she reminded herself that Gibraltar was her home, not her Alcatraz. Her family were there and their house, with its pink shutters and the intricate railings and windows of the glazed veranda, facing the sunset over the entrance to the Mediterranean. Her beloved Garrison Library was also there, and the familiar streets and the Alameda Garden, where she often strolled. During her absence she had discovered passion and love; perhaps, more importantly, she had discovered writing. She felt she had acquired all the tools to continue. She would finish her article, and then she would write others – maybe something about Goya and his etchings.

In her vulnerable condition she needed something to look forward to; it was then that Rose remembered the green Olivetti typewriter she had once admired in a shop window in Gibraltar before leaving for Spain. 'Yes,' she thought, 'that is something I dream of owning and, who knows, maybe writing will be my future.'

You, Beloved, who are all
the gardens I have ever gazed at,
longing. An open window
in a country house —, and you almost,
stepped out, pensive, to meet me.

RAINER MARIA RILKE

Published by ER Publishing 2021

First published 2020 by Danaë
6 Hill Street, London, W1J 5NF

Text © Gry Iverslien Katz

Cover painting by Astrid Iverslien

ISBN 978 1 9996950 5 7

Book design by Philip Lewis